For Dawoe and Kalsang

Snow Lion Publications
P.O. Box 6483
Ithaca, New York 14851 USA
607-273-8519
www.snowlionpub.com

Originally published in Swedish under the title *De tre silverslantarna*
by Natur och Kultur, Stockholm

Swedish text: copyright © 1994, 2011 Veronica Leo and Tashi Daknewa
English edition: copyright © 1995, 2011 Veronica Leo and Tashi Daknewa
Illustrations: copyright © 1994, 2011 Veronica Leo

Translation by Nina Åberg and Ami Kadar

Printed in Canada

ISBN-10: 1-55939-372-6
ISBN-13: 978-1-55939-372-0

Library of Congress catalog number 94-39648

Co-production rights handled by
KERSTIN KVINT Literary & Co-Production Agency
Stockholm, Sweden

The Three Silver Coins

A folk story from Tibet
told by
TASHI DAKNEWA
to
VERONICA LEO
who recreated it in words and pictures

Snow Lion Publications

Ithaca, New York

Once upon a time there was a boy named Jinpa. Together with his widowed mother he lived in a tiny cottage high in the mountains of Tibet. Since they were very poor, Jinpa helped his mother by collecting firewood, which he sold to a wealthy merchant in a nearby town. That way, they could buy the tea, tsampa and butter that made up their daily fare.

One day the merchant asked Jinpa to supply his house with firewood while he was away on business, and he promised to pay Jinpa well when he returned. Being an obedient and industrious boy, Jinpa worked hard, and he collected so much firewood that as payment he received three sparkling silver coins.

Jinpa had never seen so much money in his life and hurried home to show his mother. His mother could hardly believe her eyes. At first she even accused Jinpa of theft. But when Jinpa assured her that he had earned the silver coins through honest work, she was happy.

"Then listen, my son," said the mother. "With so much money, you can become rich. If you invest it carefully, it will increase a hundredfold. Before you is the world, full of opportunities; make the most of it. Gone will be our days of poverty, and you will not have to gather firewood anymore."

But the boy replied, "I haven't got any experience in business; my only skill is gathering firewood."

However, his mother insisted, and since Jinpa was an obedient child and wished to please his mother, he ventured into the world to seek his fortune, carrying with him his three silver coins.

Jinpa set out at a swift pace. Soon he passed an old man with a bag, and from the bag came a whining, mewing sound. Jinpa wondered what was in the bag, and asked the old man.

"Just a mangy old cat," replied the man, "which will soon be thrown in the river."

"But the cat will lose its life!" Jinpa protested.

"Boys like you should not poke into other people's business," snapped the old man. "This old cat has had its time. She's too old to catch mice, so she takes to stealing my milk instead. Enough is enough!"

Jinpa felt upset. Suddenly he had an idea: perhaps he could buy the cat for one silver coin. No sooner did he suggest this than the deal was done. Jinpa got the cat as well as the bag in the bargain, and the man took the coin and hurried away.

Immediately Jinpa released the cat. She sat down and licked her paws, and then she spoke: "If you now grant me my freedom, I promise to help you if ever the need arises."

"I have no claim on your life, so off you go," replied Jinpa. "You're your own master."

So the cat stood up and stretched, and started down the mountain. Before she disappeared from sight, she turned around and gave Jinpa a long look filled with gratitude.

Jinpa continued on his way, feeling quite pleased that he had spent his first silver coin so well.

On he strolled, and before much time had passed he came upon a man dragging a dog by a rope. The dog was struggling and whining, the man was pulling and tugging, and Jinpa couldn't keep from asking what was going on.

"I am looking for a place to tie up this wretched dog," said the man.

"But why?" asked Jinpa. "If you do, it may starve."

"That's precisely the plan," came the reply. "This dog is of no use any longer. He's old and ill-tempered, and all he can do is beg for food. Enough is enough!"

Jinpa was horrified at the cruelty of such a plan, and ventured to ask if he could buy the dog with one of his silver coins. To his surprise, the man immediately handed him the rope, took the coin and disappeared.

Jinpa lost no time in untying the bedraggled creature, which at once began wagging its tail.

"Thank you for saving my life," said the dog. "One day I shall repay you for this kind deed."

"Feel free to go wherever you please," replied Jinpa, "but take care of yourself!"

As old as he was, the dog leapt for joy. Then he trotted off, stopping now and then to look back at the boy who had saved him.

Once more Jinpa set out with a light heart. With two lucky ventures behind him, surely the third would turn out well!

It was late when he came at last to a lake where a fisherman was just pulling in his catch. Jinpa felt hungry and the promise of fish for dinner was welcome indeed, so he approached the fisherman.

"Will you sell me some fish?" he asked.

"Certainly," came the reply, "if you have any money."

Jinpa showed him the last silver coin and asked if it was enough. It was. In a twinkling the fisherman was gone and Jinpa was left standing with a big slippery fish in his arms.

Suddenly the fish gave a start, opened its mouth and whispered huskily, "My dearest boy, please release me into the water, otherwise I'll die!"

Jinpa was both startled and ashamed. What had he been thinking? To kill another creature in order to still his own hunger? He went straight to the water's edge and threw the fish as far out into the lake as he could.

For a moment it seemed as if it was already too late—the fish floated motionless at the surface. But then it splashed its tail and took a dive, only to return and raise its head out of the water.

"Thank you for letting me live! You have a good heart. If ever you need help, just come to this beach and call me, and I shall help you at once!" So saying, it plunged into the blue depths.

Jinpa stood wondering how a fish deep down in the lake could possibly help him. However that might be, he had spent his three silver coins and so he might as well return home.

That night Jinpa slept on the beach under the open sky and at dawn he arose and set off for home. It was already dark when he reached his familiar mountainside.

His mother was pleased to see him. She gave him dinner, and as soon as he had eaten she eagerly asked what he had done with his silver coins. However, to his great surprise, his mother was not at all pleased when he told her how he had saved three animals.

"A cat, a dog and a fish for three silver coins!" she cried. "And what good will that do you? Ah, what a misfortune!"

She scolded him and carried on so that Jinpa had to cover his ears. Well, she even pinched him, she was so angry.

Jinpa cried and begged her forgiveness; he couldn't understand what he had done wrong. The only thing he understood was that he wasn't welcome in his home any more, because suddenly he was out in the dark with the door slammed shut behind him. There he was, shut out of his house, and it was already late at night.

Without knowing where to go, he started walking and didn't stop until he reached the shore of the lake. He sat down in the sand near the water's edge, and tears began to stream down his cheeks.

At home his mother almost immediately regretted her outburst. She cried a little, then put the teakettle on the fire and sat down to wait, hoping that her son would return soon.

But Jinpa didn't know this as he sat by the dark lake feeling abandoned by the whole world.

Suddenly Jinpa remembered the fish that had offered to help him if ever he got into trouble.

"Fish!" he shouted. "Where are you? I need your help."

All of a sudden a clap of thunder cracked the silence and lightning cut through the glassy surface of the water. A strange figure rose slowly from the depths. It wore a crown on its head, but its lower body was that of a fish. Jinpa realized that this must be the King of the Nagas himself, ruler of the depths.

"Do not be afraid," said the King, and his voice echoed over the still lake. "You may not recognize me, since I had the form of a fish when we met before. Yes, I am the very fish you recently spared. Alas, I can tell from your face that something is troubling you. Now I want to help you, so please tell me what has happened."

And so Jinpa told him about the three silver coins, about the cat and the dog, and about how angry and disappointed his mother had been.

"She wants me to get rich!" he said.

The King of the Nagas laughed so hard it sounded like thunder between the mountains. "If that's all, don't worry. I have immeasurable riches and am pleased to share them with a decent boy like you."

So saying, the King of the Nagas disappeared into the water and soon reappeared with a bamboo stick which he held out to Jinpa.

"This is a magic wand. With it you can wish for whatever you like, whether it exists in the world or not. As you can see, it has three joints, and each joint can be parted. By opening the joints, your wishes will be fulfilled. And if you put them back together, what you have wished for will vanish. It's as simple as that, but mark my words, take good care of the wand!"

With this the King disappeared back into the blue depths, leaving Jinpa to wonder at the magic stick in his hands.

Jinpa was eager to try out his magic wand. At dawn, when the sun rose and colored the lake a deep golden red, Jinpa opened the first joint. His wish was for a big, beautiful house, because that, he thought, was exactly what a rich man should have.

A loud rumble filled the air, as if a thousand stones had rolled down the mountain. When he dared to open his eyes again, a fine house stood before him—in fact, the finest house he had ever seen. Astounded, he walked through its vast rooms, but there was nobody in sight. Jinpa realized that both riches and servants are needed to manage such a house, and so he parted the second joint of his magic wand while wishing for both money and servants.

After a few moments he could hear the jingling sound of thousands of coins—the great doors were opened and out came a long line of servants bowing and asking what their master wished. Jinpa got embarrassed; he didn't know at all what to say, especially since he had no idea how to run a house. After all, his mother had taken care of their own cottage. He decided that what he still needed was a wife who could manage the house.

So he parted the last joint and wished for a good and beautiful wife, and soon the most beautiful maiden stepped out from the house escorted by her ladies-in-waiting. She smiled at Jinpa and invited him in.

Jinpa moved into the beautiful house and lived there with his good and beautiful wife. They were very happy and never had to worry about tomorrow. The servants attended them with delicious foods, and the chests were filled with the most exquisite silk brocades. They lived like a prince and princess, with the days passing in festivity and joy, and Jinpa completely forgot about his poor mother alone on the mountain.

Now on the shore opposite Jinpa's fine house lived the mighty King Dawa Drakpa. At the sight of the impressive new palace across the lake he became very alarmed and consulted his ministers, who told him to have its owner brought to the court. That way he would be able to discover his new neighbor's intentions.

The King thought that was a good idea and assigned two generals, two ministers, some courtiers, and, to be on the safe side, three particularly brave soldiers to fetch him. When they arrived, Jinpa and his beautiful wife were already there to greet them. They were both so elegantly and expensively dressed that the King's men were filled with the deepest respect. Humbly they asked if Jinpa would care to come with them to meet the King, who, they said, would like to make the acquaintance of his noble neighbor.

"I am honored and it will be a pleasure," Jinpa replied. "Wait just one minute, while I pack my things." So saying, he took out the magic wand (which he always carried with him) and closed the first joint. The King's men were astonished to see the beautiful house disappear. Jinpa closed the second joint, and all the servants disappeared. And when he closed the last joint there wasn't a trace of either the wife or the ladies-in-waiting. There was only Jinpa, and he was once again dressed in his old, worn chuba.

"Now we can go," he said happily.

Now as soon as King Dawa Drakpa realized that Jinpa was just an ordinary boy he instantly became contemptuous.

"What tricks are you up to?" he asked harshly.

Jinpa showed him his magic wand and politely explained how it worked.

"Hand it over immediately," ordered the King, and Jinpa obliged. No sooner had the King got the stick than an evil expression came over his face. He gave a sign to the soldiers and before Jinpa knew what had happened, he was pushed out into the King's yard.

When Jinpa realized that not only had he lost his magic wand but also his beautiful wife, his home and all his wealth, tears welled up in his eyes. But what good did it do to be sad? Since he couldn't stay there, he might as well return home. He walked slowly back down to the beach and got a ferry to take him across the lake. The sun was setting behind the mountains, and Jinpa decided to stop for the night.

He was just about to fall asleep when he heard a familiar mewing sound. He looked around, and there on a nearby stone sat his old friend the cat.

"I can tell you are in trouble. Tell me what has happened and perhaps I can help you," said the cat.

The mere thought of his misfortune made Jinpa cry again, and sobbing, he told the story about the magic wand and the evil King Dawa Drakpa. The cat listened compassionately. But suddenly she arched her back and her eyes flashed with anger.

"You have indeed been wronged!" she spat. "King Dawa Drakpa has fooled you, but don't despair. I myself will see that you get your magic wand back!"

And with these bold words, she looked just like the strong and fearless snow lion.

Jinpa too plucked up courage. At dawn they started walking in the direction of the lake, and they hadn't gone very far when they saw coming towards them the old dog that Jinpa had saved. When the dog saw Jinpa, he was overjoyed and greeted him with wet dog kisses. Only after he had calmed down a little could he ask Jinpa where they were going. Once again Jinpa had to tell his sad story.

"I also want to help you," said the dog. "May I join you?"

"And how exactly do you think you can help us, if I may ask?" The cat stepped forward and eyed the dog with a haughty air.

"We'll think of something," interrupted Jinpa. "Come, let's go."

But when they reached the lake, the cat suddenly sat down and wrapped her tail around her legs. "I will wait here while you two find a boat," she said. Jinpa and the dog looked everywhere, but there was no boat to be seen.

"We shall have to swim then," said Jinpa.

The cat began to wail at the top of her lungs. When Jinpa and the dog cautiously asked what had happened, she explained that although she was usually very brave, she detested water and on no account would she swim.

"So if I cannot cross the lake, how can I help you find the magic wand?" she cried even louder.

Here the dog spoke up. "I've been wondering how I can help. Now I know. Climb on my back and I'll carry you across. You need not even get your paws wet. I will help you cross the lake so you can help Jinpa retrieve the magic wand."

And so they went. The dog took the cat on its back and swam across, and Jinpa swam beside them.

The dog had hardly reached the other side of the lake when the cat jumped ashore and sat down to lick her paws. When she had finished she deigned to address the dog.

"Thank you, you really are a good dog. But now, dear friends, I must rest because the night will be hard. Meanwhile I suggest you make yourselves useful by going to the village and begging some tsampa for our dinner. Do be careful, though, for the King must not know that we're here."

Jinpa and the dog heartily agreed and set off for the little village that lay nestled close to the palace walls. Its narrow streets were crowded with people: merchants, monks on pilgrimage and ordinary travellers from all over the country. They came to shop, to meet their friends, and to exchange news. Happiness and merriment filled the air, adding a welcome to the excitement of the marketplace. No one could resist the look on the dog's face, so Jinpa and the dog were not without food for long.

"You see," said the dog with satisfaction as they returned to the beach, "one needs so little to survive. Possessions can become a hindrance and a burden. One should live simply. Besides, today we have also given some people the chance to show their good heart, which is not only to our benefit but to theirs as well."

The cat was waiting impatiently by the lake. When they had finished their dinner, she said, "Now I've got to go. You wait here. Do not worry about me. Should I not be back by dawn, then something has gone wrong. But trust me, and sleep well. There's a reason my last owners called me the master thief!"

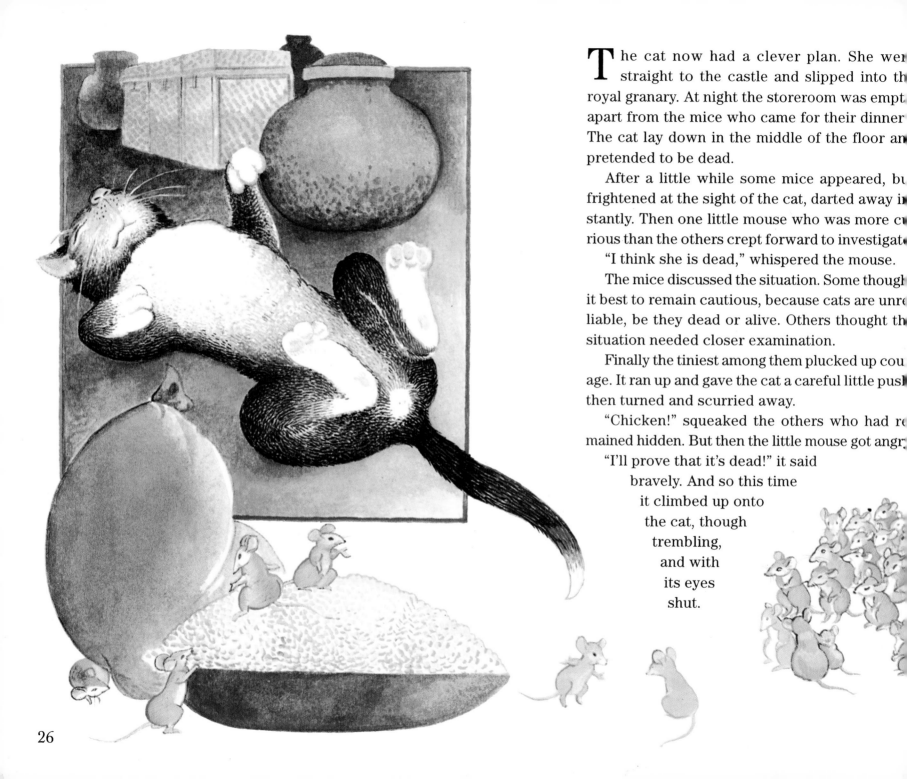

The cat now had a clever plan. She wen
straight to the castle and slipped into th
royal granary. At night the storeroom was empt
apart from the mice who came for their dinner
The cat lay down in the middle of the floor an
pretended to be dead.

After a little while some mice appeared, bu
frightened at the sight of the cat, darted away i
stantly. Then one little mouse who was more cu
rious than the others crept forward to investigat

"I think she is dead," whispered the mouse.

The mice discussed the situation. Some though
it best to remain cautious, because cats are unre
liable, be they dead or alive. Others thought th
situation needed closer examination.

Finally the tiniest among them plucked up cou
age. It ran up and gave the cat a careful little pusl
then turned and scurried away.

"Chicken!" squeaked the others who had re
mained hidden. But then the little mouse got angr

"I'll prove that it's dead!" it said
bravely. And so this time
it climbed up onto
the cat, though
trembling,
and with
its eyes
shut.

The cat did not move a limb. The tiny mouse got a good grip on one of her whiskers and pulled with all its strength. Still the cat was motionless.

Now the other mice dared to approach. One by one they climbed up on the cat, and it was not long before they were all dancing happily on top of her, rejoicing that the enemy was dead.

The cat lay dead. Never had the mice been so triumphant. They skipped about, bouncing up and down, squeaking with joy and choking with laughter.

The mice only wished for their King to come and share their joy, and some of them ran to get him. The King at first didn't want to believe them at all.

"It can be a trap," he said.

But when he saw that his subjects dared to dance on top of the cat, he was convinced and he, too, stepped up on top of the cat, though in a very dignified manner.

At this very moment the cat opened her emerald eyes and nimbly snatched the terrified King!

"Your Highness," said the cat, "do not fear. I shall not eat you immediately. Quite to the contrary, it is I who need your help. You will be free if you will do as I ask."

"O big cat, I am at your command," replied the King faintly.

"Excellent," responded the cat, and then she went on to describe the magic bamboo wand that surely was hidden somewhere in the palace. "Order your subjects to look everywhere," she continued, "and to search every nook and cranny. The magic wand must be here by sunrise, or, I am sorry to say, I will have to eat Your Highness for breakfast."

At the sound of this threat, the mouse king got pale, but he managed to call his mice together and tell them what they had to do. They plucked up their courage and were almost prepared to die for him. They promised to search through the palace and swore that they would find the magic wand before sunrise.

And so they ran off through secret passages, palace chambers and ballrooms; they checked under carpets, peered behind curtains, opened all coffers, boxes and drawers: but the wand was nowhere to be found.

There was only one room left—the wicked King's bedroom. The very bravest mice slipped through the door. The King was sleeping, but from under his pillow a long box poked out.

How brave those mice were! Right next to the King's ear they nibbled a hole in the box. And how happy they were when soon they saw the magic wand! With pounding hearts, they managed to pull it out of the box and maneuver it into the tiny mouse hole under the bed. Then began the long and difficult journey through the narrow, winding passageways where the wand repeatedly threatened to get stuck.

The King of Mice had long since fainted from tension when the mice arrived, dishevelled and tired, pulling the magic wand. They placed it at the feet of the cat.

The cat was true to her word and immediately released the King of the Mice. She took the magic wand between her teeth and stole out of the palace the same way she had arrived. She went straight down to the lakeside where Jinpa and the dog were still sleeping and there delivered the magic wand to her old friend. When Jinpa awoke and saw the wand he could not believe his eyes and wanted to hear over and over again how the cat had outsmarted the mice and got them to search for the magic wand. Finally the cat had to tell Jinpa that she had had enough. Now it was time to wish back the house, the servants, and the wife. Then she wanted some milk and some peace and quiet.

"Of course," answered Jinpa, "but not exactly here, because you never know what the wicked King may do. It's better if we go home to my mother's place. There on the mountain we can live in peace."

The two animals agreed at once. They returned the same way they had come and by evening they had reached Jinpa's old cottage.

What joy! His mother cried for happiness, but when she started to prepare dinner, Jinpa said, "No, Mother, let me."

And he brought out the magic wand. With roaring thunder, lightning and the jingle as of a thousand coins, there was the house again with all its servants. Jinpa took his mother by the hand and entered the house.

"Oh, my son, if only you had a wife to share all this with," said his mother.

Then he parted the last joint of the wand. A blinding light filled the room, and there she was again, his good and beautiful wife.

From that day on they lived together with the good old dog and the wise cat in the beautiful house. Jinpa's mother never had to worry again, and with time Jinpa and his wife had four happy children. And Jinpa, who had everything he needed, could now help others who had less. But the magic wand he hid carefully, because one thing was sure, he would never again wish away his home or family!

And so ends the story about the three silver coins, a story Tashi heard when he was a little boy and which he in turn told to his sons Dawoe and Kalsang. Kalsang is in the picture here.

This story comes from Tibet where Tashi was born. Tibet is often called the Roof of the World, because it is so high up in the mountains that the highest peaks reach all the way to the sky.

In Tibet everyone learns that all life is sacred, even the lives of animals. To show compassion and to offer help where it is needed is the most important thing in life. Jinpa did this, and therefore he fared so well, explains Tashi.

Glossary

A *chuba* is the full-length robe worn by Tibetan men and women.

Nagas live in the deep waters. They are half human and half fish, and are said to be extremely wealthy.

The *snow lion* is the national symbol of Tibet. According to legend, it is a powerful and fearless animal that lives in the mountains.

Tsampa is roasted barley flour. It is the main food of Tibetans, and is often mixed with tea to make a tasty porridge.